XX 0582 **417929** 8007

ITEMS SHOULD BE RETURNED ON OR BEFORE THE LAST DATE
SHOWN BELOW. ITEMS NOT ALREADY REQUESTED BY OTHER
READERS MAY BE RENEWED BY PERSONAL APPLICATION, BY
WRITING, OR BY TELEPHONE. TO RENEW, <u>GIVE THE DATE DUE
AND THE NUMBER ON THE BARCODE LABEL</u>.

FINES CHARGED FOR OVERDUE ITEMS WILL INCLUDE
POSTAGE INCURRED IN RECOVERY. DAMAGE TO, OR LOSS
OF ITEMS WILL BE CHARGED TO THE BORROWER.

LEABHARLANNA POIBLÍ CHATHAIR BHAILE ÁTHA CLIATH
DUBLIN CITY PUBLIC LIBRARIES

Dublin City
Baile Átha Cliath

Ballyfermot Branch Tel. 6269324 / 5

Date Due	Date Due	Date Due

Pearson Education Limited
Edinburgh Gate, Harlow,
Essex CM20 2JE, England
and Associated Companies throughout the world.

ISBN 0 582 41792 9

First published in the USA by Delacorte Press 1990
Published simultaneously in Canada
First published by Penguin Books 1991
This adaptation first published by Penguin Books 1997
Published by Addison Wesley Longman Limited and Penguin Books Ltd. 1998
New edition first published 1999

Text copyright © Donald Domonkos 1997
Illustrations copyright © Bob Harvey 1997
All rights reserved

The moral right of the adapter and of the illustrator has been asserted

Set in 11/14pt Monotype Bembo by
Rowland Phototypesetting Ltd,
Bury St Edmunds, Suffolk
Printed in Spain by Mateu Cromo, S.A. Pinto (Madrid)

*All rights reserved; no part of this publication may be reproduced, stored
in a retrieval system, or transmitted in any form or by any means,
electronic, mechanical, photocopying, recording or otherwise, without the
prior written permission of the Publishers.*

Published by Pearson Education Limited in association with
Penguin Books Ltd., both companies being subsidiaries of Pearson Plc

For a complete list of the titles available in the Penguin Readers series please write to your
local Pearson Education office or to: Marketing Department, Penguin Longman Publishing,
5 Bentinck Street, London W1M 5RN.

Contents

Introduction

Ronnie said, "What is this? Where's our money, Harry? Do you have it? I want to see it."

Chili said to the little rich boy, "Hey, Ronnie, look at me."

This surprised Ronnie. He looked at Chili. So did Catlett. "You bought a piece of a movie, Ronnie. You didn't buy a piece of Harry. He'll make your movie. You heard him. You understand? We're doing another movie first. That's how it is."

"Who are you?" Ronnie said in an ugly voice.

"I'm the man who's telling you the news, Ronnie."

In Miami, Chili Palmer was a gangster. He's in Hollywood now, helping his new friend Harry Zimm to make a movie. But the movie business is as dangerous as Chili's old business. A new enemy wants him out of the way and an old enemy hasn't forgotten him. It's getting "hot" in Hollywood.

Elmore Leonard is one of America's favorite crime writers. He was born in New Orleans in 1925, but grew up near Detroit. His first book, *The Bounty Hunters*, came out in 1953. His fifth book, *Hombre*, was made into a movie in 1967 with Paul Newman. He wrote his first crime story, *The Bounce*, in 1969. His other books include *Stick* (1983) and *Glitz* (1985). *Get Shorty* (1990) is his twenty-eighth book.

The movie of *Get Shorty* came to the cinemas in 1996 and was a great success. It was an important movie for John Travolta. He was a successful actor and dancer in the 1970s with *Saturday Night Fever* (1977) and *Grease* (1978), but he was less popular in the 1980s. People noticed him again in Quentin Tarantino's *Pulp Fiction* (1994), but some people think that he is even better as Chili Palmer in *Get Shorty*. Travolta is now one of the most successful actors in Hollywood.

Get Shorty

The trouble between Chili Palmer and Ray Bones started in Miami. Ray took Chili's jacket. Chili was eating lunch with his friend Tommy. When they finished, Chili went to get his jacket. It wasn't there.

"Who took it?"

"Mr Ray Barboni," the man said. "He didn't take it. He just borrowed it."

"Really?" Chili said.

Tommy knew Ray Barboni's house. He also knew Ray Barboni.

"They call him Ray Bones. He works for Jimmy Cap." Tommy stopped the car in front of Ray's house. "And you know Jimmy Cap, so get the jacket but don't make Ray mad, okay?"

Chili got out of the car. "Don't worry. I won't say anything to him." And he didn't. When Ray opened the door, Chili hit him in the face, walked in and got his jacket, and walked out.

Chili Palmer worked for Momo as a shylock★. People borrowed money from Chili. He always told them "Do you really want this money? I'm not a bank. If you don't pay me, well . . ." He never told them more than that, and they always paid him. It was his eyes. Chili had very cold eyes.

And Ray Bones had a broken nose. Chili Palmer was in his office a few days later when Ray Bones walked in with a gun. But Chili had a gun too. They started shooting at the same time. Ray missed and Chili didn't. The bullet hit the top of Ray's head, two inches too high to kill him.

Jimmy Cap and Momo heard about the problem between

★ A shylock is a special kind of gangster. If you borrow money from him, you have to pay him much more than he gave you.

Ray and Chili and told them both to end it. It was over. And it stayed that way for twelve years. Until someone killed Momo in New York and Jimmy Cap got his business in Miami.

This time, Ray didn't come with a gun. He didn't have to. He brought a big black man. Chili was at the hairdresser when they found him. "Hey Ray," Chili said, "these guys can cut your hair so that ugly line doesn't show." And he pointed at the long line through his hair, from the bullet.

Ray didn't laugh. "This guy," he said to the black man, "doesn't know that he's out of work. I want to see the books, Palmer."

Chili showed him the names of the people who borrowed money.

"What's this?" Ray asked, his finger on the name Leo Devoe. "He hasn't paid."

"He died," Chili said. "Airplane crash. It was in the newspaper."

"Maybe his wife has money. I don't care. Get it from her or pay it from your pocket. These are my books now. This is my money now, so you get it."

As the two men left, Chili said, "You know that jacket, Ray? I gave it to the poor two years ago."

"What jacket?" Bones said, but he knew.

Chili went to see Leo Devoe's wife. I can ask her, he thought. But he didn't. He didn't because when he went to see her, she told him, "I'm sorry that he's not dead."

Chili didn't say anything. Don't talk when you don't have to.

"They gave me money because of the crash. Three hundred thousand dollars. Leo took it. I trust you, Chili, even if you are a gangster. You find Leo and the money, and I'll give you half."

"He died," Chili said. "I read it in the newspaper."

"No," she said, "his suitcase died." And she told Chili everything that happened. It was a good story.

◆

2

*"What's this?" Ray asked, his finger on the name
of Leo Devoe. "He hasn't paid."*

Harry Zimm closed his eyes again. The sounds will stop in a minute, he thought. Then we can go back to sleep.

But Karen couldn't leave it alone. "Wake up, Harry. Somebody's downstairs."

"I don't hear anything." It was true, he couldn't hear anything now.

"There are voices, Harry. People talking. On television. Someone came in and turned the TV on. Listen, will you?"

"Maybe it's the dog," Harry said.

"I don't have a dog," Karen said. "Now, are you going down, or do you want me to?"

Harry got out of bed and put on a T-shirt. Coming down the stairs, he could hear the TV. Probably one of Karen's actor friends trying to be funny.

The television was in the next room. Harry opened the door. The blue light from the television disappeared and the light on the desk went on. A guy that Harry didn't know was sitting there. A guy in black. Dark hair, dark eyes.

He said "Harry Zimm, how are you doing?" in a quiet voice.

"I'm Chili Palmer." The man's dark eyes stayed on him. "Where have you been, Harry?"

"Have we met?" Harry asked.

"We just did. I told you, my name's Chili Palmer. Come over here and talk to me, Harry."

The guy wasn't bad, Harry thought. Not a bad actor. He said "Harry, you looking at me?"

"I'm looking at you," Harry said, "but I don't have a script, so I don't know what you're talking about."

"You don't have a script," Chili said. "Well, do you maybe have a hundred and fifty thousand dollars? You remember Las Vegas, don't you, November of last year?"

Now Harry wasn't sure. Was this real? "How far do you want to go with this?"

The guy held out his hands. "We're there, Harry. Las Vegas. You owe Dick Allen a hundred and fifty thousand."

A guy that Harry didn't know was sitting there.
A guy in black. Dark hair, dark eyes.

This wasn't a script. Harry said "What is this? I thought that you were an actor."

The guy almost smiled. "Is that right? That I was acting?"

Harry picked up the phone. "We'll see about this."

Chili said "Harry, stop and think a minute, okay? It's hard to be a big, strong guy, a dangerous guy, Harry, when you're standing there without any pants on. Talk to me, Harry."

And Harry talked to him. He lost most of the money on a football game, he said, and then he lost the rest of it on cards.

"Trying to get your money back, right? But when you have to win, Harry, that's when you lose. Everybody knows that. And from what I hear, Harry, maybe the money wasn't yours. Maybe it was for a movie."

"Maybe, maybe . . . maybe you don't know what you're talking about," Harry said. "I'll pay Dick Allen, I'll call him tomorrow. Now, can I call you a cab, go back to bed?"

The guy didn't want a cab. He said, "So you make movies?"

"That's what I do," Harry said.

Chili said, "I think I got an idea for one, for a movie."

And Harry said, "Yeah? What's it about?"

◆

Karen was worried. She came out of the bedroom and stood at the top of the stairs, listening. She heard Harry's voice. He was saying "Can I call you a cab?" And then something she couldn't hear, and then Harry's voice again. "Yeah? What's it about?" Hollywood's favorite words. Someone was selling an idea. She waited a minute and then she came down the stairs.

They were drinking together when she came into the room.

"Karen," Harry said, "say hello to Chili Palmer. Dick Allen sent him. Chili, this is Karen Weir."

"Karen Flores," she said.

"That's right," Harry said. "You changed your name back."

Chili looked at her and saw a very pretty woman. Not like in her movies, but still pretty. "Karen," he said, "it's nice to meet you."

6

"He's telling me an idea for a movie," Harry said. "It's not bad. Tell Karen, see what she thinks."

"You want me to start over?" Chili asked.

"How did you get into my house?" Karen asked him.

"The back door. It was open. I mean that it wasn't locked."

"So you just walked in?" But she didn't sound mad.

"You want to hear his idea?" Harry said. "This guy, everybody thinks he's dead, they even pay his wife because he died in this crash. Go on, tell her."

"He owes money to a shylock," Chili began. "He can't pay and he's scared. He wants to get away. He buys an airplane ticket. But there's a problem at the airport, he doesn't get on the airplane. His suitcase goes on but he's in the bar when the airplane leaves. And he's still in the bar when the airplane crashes, killing everyone. His luck has changed, he thinks. He's dead. He doesn't have to pay the shylock. Then some people from the airplane company come to see his wife. They tell her that they're very sorry about her husband and they give her a lot of money. The guy takes the money and goes to Las Vegas. There he wins more money and he comes here to Los Angeles. After that, I don't know what happens."

"That's it?" Harry asked. "That's your great idea for a movie? That's half a movie, with holes in it. Some of it is good, but . . . they just give the wife the money?"

Karen smiled. "Harry doesn't realise that it's a true story. The airplane crash in Florida, I read about it in the newspaper."

"That's where you got the idea," Harry said to Chili. "And then you thought of the rest."

"No, Harry, it's all true, everything that I told you."

Harry said, "Wait a minute. You're not the guy, are you? No, you work for Dick Allen. Dick Allen wants him."

"Dick Allen wants you, Harry. He wants you to pay him. But I am looking for the guy."

"Harry," Karen said, "maybe you still haven't woken up. He's the shylock, Harry."

7

Harry didn't say anything at first. Then he started talking about Chili's idea again. "You know what the problem is? There's no good guy in the story."

Chili said, "The shylock's the good guy." And to explain this, he told them about Ray Bones.

When he finished, Karen said goodnight and went back to bed. Harry wanted to talk more. He asked Chili, "Your work is dangerous, isn't it? I mean, the trouble with Ray Bones . . ."

"He still wants to kill me," Chili said.

"And he doesn't know about Leo Devoe, does he?"

Chili said no.

"You carry a gun, don't you?"

Chili looked at Harry. There was a little smile on Chili's face. "Harry," he said, "you're asking a lot of questions. You want me to do something for you, ask me." And when Harry didn't say anything, Chili said, "Listen, when I came to L.A., I asked people about you. Dick Allen isn't your only problem, is he? Other people want their money too, right?"

Harry said, "Look, these guys came to me. They've put money into two of my movies. They were very happy with them. So they wanted to put money into another one. It'll be a good movie."

"Harry, you took their money and you lost it. You haven't told them about it. Why not?"

"Because," Harry said, "these guys scare me."

"Then why did you take their money to Las Vegas?"

"I had to. There's another movie. A great script. I need half a million dollars to start."

"And these guys? Why not ask them?"

No, Harry said, he didn't want to. The wrong people for this movie. This movie was too big.

"Then what's the problem?"

"I told you," Harry said. "The money. I need a star. I know the perfect man. But a meeting with him costs half a million dollars."

"Who's the man?" Chili asked.

"Michael Weir."

Chili said, "Yeah, he's good. He played the gangster in that movie, *The Cyclone*, didn't he? I like him. Have you talked to him?"

"He's seen the script. I sent it to him. But I can't talk to him about it. Not without half a million dollars. That's Hollywood. So I thought about Karen. She was married to him, did you know that? He'll listen to her if she asks."

"You asked her?"

"No, I can't. I ask her and she'll say no. It has to be her idea. Then she'll do it."

"Maybe I can ask him," Chili said. "Get your meeting for you. Or maybe you're thinking about Leo's money. Ask him, Leo, you want to put money in a movie or you want to go to prison? Something like that? Having Leo in the movie, that's better than having those guys? The ones that scare you?"

Harry didn't say anything but Chili understood. "I can talk to the guys. Tell them to wait. If you want, Harry."

When Harry went back to bed, Karen was still awake. "Did your new friend leave, Harry?"

"No, I put him in the room behind the kitchen. He's sleeping."

"Harry," Karen said, "the guy's a gangster."

"Then," said Harry, "he came to the right town, didn't he?"

◆

Harry took Chili to his office the next day. Chili promised to help him, but Harry had to listen. "First, you don't tell them my name. You just start talking to them. You don't tell them about the other movie. You can't make their movie now. You'll make it later. Don't explain. Right? Now, tell me about them."

"There are two of them. Ronnie Wingate is a little rich boy, he likes to play with guns. Bo Catlett is the other guy. He doesn't talk much. Wears nice clothes. He's Mexican or something, I don't know."

9

Chili was looking at the photographs on the office walls.
There was a good one of Karen.

Chili was looking at the photographs on the office walls. There was a good one of Karen. He was thinking, there's something about her, and then Harry said, "They're here."

Chili stayed where he was, at the desk. Ronnie Wingate came in first, looked at Chili, looked away. "Hey, Harry, what year is it in here?" he said, looking at the furniture and the photographs.

The other one, Bo Catlett, was taller than Ronnie and he was black. His skin wasn't very dark, not much darker than his shirt, but he was black. Bo sat down and said, "How are you?" to Chili. "What brings you here?"

"The movies," Chili said.

"This is my friend Chili Palmer," Harry said. Wonderful, Chili thought, Harry's already forgetting.

"Where have you been, Harry?" Ronnie asked. "Three months and you haven't called."

New York, Harry said. "I had some business there. But there's no problem, I'll make the movie. A little later than I thought, maybe in the spring."

Ronnie didn't like it. "What are you telling us, Harry?"

Chili held up his hand. "Harry? Harry, you're going to make their movie, aren't you?"

"Yeah," Harry said. "But I have to make another movie first. I promised this guy. Years ago."

Chili wanted to hit Harry. Don't explain and don't talk about the other movie.

Ronnie said "What is this? Where's our money, Harry? Do you have it? I want to see it."

Chili said to the little rich boy "Hey, Ronnie, look at me."

This surprised Ronnie. He looked at Chili. So did Catlett.

"You bought a piece of a movie, Ronnie. You didn't buy a piece of Harry. He'll make your movie. You heard him. You understand? We're doing another movie first. That's how it is."

"Who are you?" Ronnie said in an ugly voice.

"I'm the man who's telling you the news, Ronnie."

11

Ronnie turned to Bo Catlett. "Bo? . . ."

Chili looked at Bo now. Bo asked Harry, "What's the other movie?"

Chili said, "Harry, I'll answer that question. But first, am I talking to you or am I talking to him?" he said, looking at Ronnie.

Bo said, "You can talk to me."

"That's what I thought," Chili said. "The other movie? That's not your business." And he kept his cold eyes on him.

Now it was between the two of them. Until Harry picked up the script and said "This is it. *Mr Lovejoy*. It's nothing. Not your kind of movie."

"I don't know," Bo said. "Why not put our money in that one? What's the problem?"

"I'll think about it," Harry said.

◆

After Bo Catlett left Harry Zimm's office, he went home and changed his clothes. Bo changed clothes two or three times a day. He liked to look nice. Then he drove to the airport.

Bo had a ticket but he wasn't going anywhere. He was waiting for someone. The Bear was with him. Bo was thinking about Chili Palmer and the Bear. Mr Palmer, meet the Bear. The Bear was a very big man.

Bo and the Bear were waiting for Yayo. Yayo was nobody but Yayo had something for them. And they had one hundred and seventy thousand dollars for Yayo. The money was in a locker right here at the airport.

Now Bo saw Yayo. The man was pushing people out of his way, a little gangster, very dangerous. Bo hated these guys. All of them like actors from the gangster movies.

The Bear disappeared. He was getting Yayo's suitcase. Yayo was walking towards Bo, towards his money. Bo looked to the right and the left. He saw them then. A man by the door. Another one on the other side of the room. Policemen.

Yayo said, "Hey, where's the money?"

Ronnie turned to Bo Catlett. "Bo?"

Bo said quietly "Don't talk to me. You're waiting for someone. Don't look at me. I'm going to sit down. When I get up, you sit in my chair. There will be a key on the chair. The money is in a locker. But don't go near it now. Wait. They're watching us. You understand? Not now."

Chili Palmer was talking on the telephone to his friend Tommy. He was asking questions about Michael Weir. "Some of the guys met him," Tommy was saying, "when he made that movie *Cyclone*. He came down to 86th Street. Wanted to see real gangsters. But forget Weir, Chili. You have other problems. Ray Bones is coming out to L.A."

"He knows I'm here?"

"Yeah," Tommy said, "I told him but he already knew. He talked to Leo Devoe's wife, what's her name, Fay?"

After he talked to Tommy, Chili called Fay. "I had to tell him, Chili," Fay said. "He hit me. I didn't want him to hit me again. Now everyone will know about Leo, won't they?"

Chili said no, he didn't think so. "Bones wants the money for himself."

When he put down the telephone, Harry showed him something in an old newspaper. It was Michael Weir with his new girl-friend. Chili looked carefully at the photograph. He knew Michael Weir's face from the movies but he knew the other face, too. What was her name?

"Nicki," Harry said.

Not Nicki then, Chili thought. Nicole, a singer from Miami. "I know her. Where's she playing these days?"

Harry said, "I'll ask some people."

Chili thought of something else. "Hey, Harry, I haven't read this script. Do you have it here?"

Harry said no. He gave Chili his office keys. "It's on the desk. Remember to lock the door when you leave."

But when he got to the office, Chili didn't need the key. The door was open. Bo Catlett was sitting at the desk. Bo looked up and said "This isn't bad, you know? This *Mr Lovejoy*."

14

He knew Michael Weir's face from the movies but he knew the other face too. What was her name?

Chili said nothing. He was thinking, how did he get in here?

"Harry lied. He said the script was no good but he was holding it like gold, wasn't he? So I had to read it. Now, tell me if I'm wrong. Harry doesn't want our money in this movie because he has your money. Not quite yours; gangster money, I mean. I asked people about you. You're not in the movie business."

Chili said, "I am now."

Bo smiled. "Can I ask you — who will play *Lovejoy*? Who's your star?"

Chili said, "We're getting Michael Weir."

"How are you doing that?"

"I put a gun right here," Chili said, touching the side of his head, "and I tell him 'Put your name on the bottom line, Mike, or you're dead.'"

Bo laughed. "Yeah, good idea, no more difficult actors. Tell me, have you read this?"

Chili said no, not all of it.

"Read it now. Then we can talk about it, okay? I have some ideas. It's good, but we can make it better."

Why not, Chili thought. I came here to read it, didn't I?

◆

When Bo Catlett returned home, the Bear was waiting for him. "We have a problem" the Bear said. "Yayo. He's still at the airport. Won't go near the money. The police are still there."

"Then we have two problems. The other one is this guy Chili Palmer." He told the Bear about Chili and the movie. "Is he a real gangster, or is he another Yayo?"

"One Yayo is enough," the Bear said. "You want me to go to the airport, bring the little bad guy back to the office?"

"Yeah, go get him."

The Bear left. Bo drove to the office, thinking about movies and money. Living like the rich. Soon, he thought. Very soon. He parked in the garage and waited in his car.

"Where's my money?" It was the first thing Yayo said when he got out of the Bear's car.

16

"Yayo," Bo said calmly, "you know where it is. You know the problem. So you wait a day, okay?"

In a loud voice the smaller man said "No, it's not okay. Maybe I just go to the locker, take the money now. The police, they catch me, I tell them about you."

Catlett said "Yeah? You wait here a minute, I'll be back." He left them and went to Ronnie's office. Where was it? He found it in the desk. He came back to the garage with the gun in his hand, his arm straight out.

"What are you doing?" Yayo said, his voice still loud.

"I'm saying goodbye, Yayo," Catlett said, and shot him in the head. "Now is it okay?" he asked Yayo.

The Bear looked down at the body. "You've done this before, haven't you?" he said.

"Not in a long time," Catlett said.

◆

Chili didn't like the place much. The crowd was too young. He asked the barman about Nicki.

"She's downstairs. You in music?"

"Movies," Chili said, walking towards the stairs.

The room was almost empty downstairs. There were four guys at the far end but he didn't see Nicki anywhere. He made a small sound and they turned to look at him. The one in the middle said "Chili?"

It was Nicole, Nicki. She ran over and gave him a kiss. "It's Chili, guys. From Miami. He's a gangster, a real gangster!" She smiled.

"So you remember me," Chili said.

"Do I remember you? You were the nicest guy at Momo's nightclub. What are you doing here?"

"I'm making a movie," Chili said. "And you live with a movie star."

"Michael, yeah. He's coming later. You want to meet him?" Just like that.

"Yeah," said Chili calmly, "why not?"

17

The room was quiet. He looked over.
Michael Weir was standing there.

Nicki gave him another kiss and went back to the others. Chili listened while they played. They were good. Suddenly the music stopped. The room was quiet. He looked over. Michael Weir was standing there.

Nicki took Weir's arm and she started to walk. Now Weir was standing in front of him. "Chili? Meet Michael Weir."

Chili stood up and put out his hand. Hey, Chili thought, this guy is short.

Michael sat down with him. "We've met before," Chili said. "Maybe you don't remember. In Brooklyn, at a club on 86th Street. You were making *The Cyclone*. You wanted to talk to some of the guys."

"That's right," Michael said. "But not really to talk, to listen. How you guys talk. I mean, I was playing a gangster, wasn't I? I had to talk like one."

"How do we talk?" Chili asked.

"Not the voices. What your voices say. 'My way is the only way.' That's how you think, isn't it? When I listen to people carefully, I understand them. I know what they're thinking."

"Really? You know what I'm thinking?"

Michael laughed. "No, I don't. But I'm interested."

"I'm thinking about a movie," Chili said.

"One of mine?"

"You've read it. You liked it. We want you to be in it."

Michael said, "Wait a minute. Sorry. I can't talk about this. There are rules, I'm sorry, I didn't make them."

"I know what you think. You see me, you think 'gangster money' I'm out of that. I was a shylock but I walked out. This is clean money, Hollywood money."

"You walked out?" Michael asked. "Why? What happened? Hurting people; you didn't like that? Scaring people?"

"I did my job. People borrow money, people have to give it back. That was my job. You, you're an actor. You play other people. Okay, play me. You're a shylock. Someone takes fifteen thousand dollars and disappears. What do you do?"

19

Chili watched Michael. The actor was thinking. "Are you the shylock now?" Chili asked.

"Yeah. Guy takes my money. I'm going to find him, take it back."

"Try it again," Chili said. "Look at me."

"I'm looking at you."

"Not the way I'm looking at you. Put it in your eyes. 'You're mine. I don't like you but I don't hate you: this is business.'"

Michael's eyes turned cold. "You? You're nothing."

"That's very good," Chili said.

"Yeah, but I find the guy?"

So Chili had to tell him the story.

"This really happened, didn't it?" Michael said. "It's a true story. You're the shylock."

"I was the shylock."

Michael was waiting for more. "Go on."

"I can't tell you more."

Michael looked at him. "Wonderful. You're wonderful. Now I have to read the script, don't I? Very clever."

"That's not the movie," Chili said. "The movie is *Mr Lovejoy*. You've read it."

"Yes, I remember. Harry Zimm's script." The actor looked over at Nicki. She was waiting for him. "Listen, I have to go. I liked *Lovejoy*."

"Can we talk about it again?"

"Anytime," Michael said. "Anytime Harry Zimm has half a million dollars."

An hour later Chili was in his hotel room making phone calls. He called Tommy first. "Sorry about this," Tommy said.

"About what?"

"Ray Bones. He'll be there tomorrow. Twelve o'clock."

◆

Bo Catlett was talking to the Bear. He was talking about movies. The Bear wasn't interested.

Michael's eyes turned cold. "You? You're nothing."

"It's a big one, Bear. They've got Michael Weir. Harry doesn't want us? Too bad. Chili Palmer doesn't want us. That Palmer, he's the problem. You listening, Bear?"

"I'm listening," the big man said. "I'll tell you one thing. You shoot Chili Palmer, you'll never see me again."

"I don't want to shoot him," Bo said. "No, I have another idea. The money at the airport. We can't touch it. Maybe Chili will go and get it for us."

"The police are waiting there," the Bear said. "Anybody tries to get that money . . ."

"That's right," Bo said. "Goodbye, Chili Palmer."

◆

After the Bear left, Bo went to the office. Marcella, the secretary, had some very good news. "Harry Zimm called. I told him to call again."

Bo took the call in Ronnie's office. "Harry, how are you?"

"I'm fine. Working on that movie, you know, *Lovejoy*."

"Yeah. Michael Weir, right?"

"This town, everybody hears everything," Harry said.

"How can I help you, Harry?"

"I need some money. Two hundred and fifty thousand."

"Harry, we gave you money. Remember?"

"I can't use that," Harry said.

Because you don't have it, Bo thought. You lost it. Forget it, he told himself. *Lovejoy* was more important. "Harry, let's have a drink. I have some money for you. I want part of this movie, Harry. It's a great script."

"You've read it?" Harry asked.

"Meet me for a drink, Harry. We'll talk. At *Tribeca's*, in an hour?"

◆

"Where's Harry?" Chili asked Karen. They were at her house.

"He made a phone call and left."

"He's not happy with me," Chili said. He wasn't really think-ing about Harry. He was looking at Karen. It was nice, sitting

*He wasn't really thinking about Harry. He was looking
at Karen.*

here with her. The sun was going down, the sky was pretty. She was too.

"He wants Michael. But Michael means money. That's where he is. Those guys with the money for the other movie."

"Catlett? He went to see Catlett?" Chili put down his drink. "Do you know where?"

"*Tribeca's*, I think. A place on Beverly Drive. Why?"

"Are you hungry?" Chili asked. "It's a restaurant, isn't it?"

"Harry's a big boy," Karen said. She thought about it. "Isn't he?"

Chili stood up. He said, "You ready?"

◆

Harry was asking about the script. "How did you see it?"

Bo smiled. "That was strange. Your man called me, I went to your office."

"My man?" Harry asked.

"Chili Palmer from Miami. Don't know why. Tell me, Harry, what does he do for you?"

"Not much," said Harry in an angry voice. Bo liked that.

"See, I know what he is. He says he's in the movie business, but he's not. He's in the trouble business. And I don't understand. Why do you need him? Has Ronnie given you trouble? I know I haven't. I've given you money. And I want to give you more. One hundred and seventy thousand dollars, it's yours. It's sitting at the airport, waiting for you."

Harry looked at him. "The airport?"

"Money from my other business, Harry. You don't want to know more. You go there, take it, it's yours. But there's a little problem. Lots of people at an airport, not all of them passengers or pilots."

"You mean the police," Harry said.

"That's possible too. Or other people. You don't want to get hurt."

Harry said no, he didn't. But he did want the money.

"I have an idea, Harry. You send Chili Palmer. He opens the locker, brings you the money. Somebody hits him on the head, you lose nothing. It's not your head."

At the same time, Chili and Karen were standing downstairs.

They looked at the bar and the tables in front of it, but Harry wasn't there. Chili started up the stairs.

A man was waiting for him at the top of the stairs, a very big man in a bright shirt. He was in the way and he wasn't moving. What's this, Chili thought, and then he saw Bo Catlett behind the big man.

Catlett said, "I'd like you to meet the Bear. He's a movie stuntman. He picks up and throws out things I don't want. Like you. Go home, Palmer. Go back to Miami."

The Bear said, "Go home while you can still walk."

Chili was standing below the Bear. He looked at him now and said, "So you're a stuntman. Are you good at your work?"

The Bear smiled and turned his head towards Bo. He didn't see Chili's hand when it moved, but he felt it. Chili's fingers closed hard between the Bear's legs. Chili pulled and the Bear screamed and fell down the stairs. Chili watched him and then he turned to Catlett. "Not bad, for a big man."

At the table, Harry asked Chili, "What was that?"

"They don't like me. Why are you here?"

"Money," Harry explained. "Bo is giving me one hundred and seventy thousand. It's in a locker at the airport."

"The airport?" Chili said. "You're not thinking, Harry. He's not giving you money, he's giving you a trip to prison. Don't go near that locker."

"Yeah, Bo said that too. He told me to send you."

Chili smiled. "That man really doesn't like me. Okay, Harry, give me the key. I'll go to the airport and see. If I don't see a problem, I'll bring you the money."

Harry put the key on the table and Chili picked it up. "It's a lot of money," Harry said. "Don't disappear with it."

After Harry left, Karen said "Oh, I forgot. One of your friends called the house. His name was . . ."

"Tommy?"

"No, not Tommy," she said. "Ray something. Ray Barboni?"

◆

Chili drove to the airport the next day. He left the locker key in his hotel room. It was ten-thirty in the morning and the airport was busy. He didn't like that, too many people. He looked at the lockers. His locker was C-018. He walked past it.

He went to the airport shop and bought a T-shirt and a bag. He put the shirt in the bag. There was a young man there who was reading the newspapers. Chili asked him "Hey, you want to make five dollars in two minutes? Go to the lockers and put this in C-017. It's a surprise for my wife."

The young man took the bag and came back with the key.

Now Chili waited. I can't see them, he thought, but the police are here. They're watching locker C-018. He waited until there was a group of people in front of the locker. He walked behind them, opened locker C-017, and took out the bag. The people walked past him. He started to walk away and two men stopped him. "Please come with us, sir."

They took Chili to a small room. They opened the bag and pulled out the shirt. That was all that was in it. They looked in his pockets. Chili said "What is this?"

"What locker did you use, sir?"

"C-sixteen or seventeen. What's the problem?"

"You're from Miami. Why are you in Los Angeles?"

"I'm in the movie business. I just started. What are you looking for?"

"Something in one of the lockers," one of the policemen said.

"Well, I don't have it, do I?" Chili said. "Can I go now?"

After he left the police, Chili went to the garage. The stunt-man was waiting for him, standing next to Chili's car.

He looked at the lockers. His locker was C-018.
He walked past it.

"You didn't have the key with you," the Bear said.

"These ideas work better when they're a surprise. Can you remember that?" He looked at the Bear. The guy wasn't very good at this work. "Tell me, what movies were you in? Maybe I've seen some of them."

The Bear said, "I need the key. Bo wants it back."

Chili laughed. "You guys are great. You give me to the police, it doesn't work, and you want your key back? You always do business like this? In Miami, people as stupid as you, they kill them. Now get away from my car."

The Bear didn't move. Chili looked down at the garage floor and then suddenly kicked the Bear in the left knee. The Bear's head came down and Chili pulled him by the hair. Chili's knee found the Bear's face. The Bear's head came back up, and Chili hit him as hard as he could in the stomach. The Bear went down.

"Here," Chili said, "put your arms like this. That's it."

The Bear felt a little better. It didn't hurt as much as before. "Hey," Chili said. "Look at me. Tell Bo, I don't want to see him again. You understand?"

The Bear opened and closed his eyes.

"You were in the movies," Chili said. "A real stuntman. What can Bo give you?" After a minute he asked "You okay?"

"Not too bad," the Bear said.

"Get another job," Chili said. "Go back to the movies."

The Bear didn't say anything. He was thinking about it.

♦

Chili drove back to his hotel. He liked the hotel. The food was good and the room was nice. They cleaned the room every afternoon.

But it was still morning. So it can't be the cleaning woman, he thought. Someone was in his room. He felt it. He opened the door and said, "Hey, Bones? I'm home."

Ray Bones was standing in the middle of the room. He had

a gun in one hand and Chili's suitcase in the other. "Get over by the chair," Ray said.

"You don't need that," Chili said, looking at the gun. "And I didn't find Leo."

"Really?" Ray said. He put the suitcase on the bed. "So what's this?" He held up a small key. "C-018." He was smiling. "A locker key. Yeah, but where's the locker?"

Chili sat down slowly on the chair. He took out a cigarette and said, "It's at the airport." It was that easy.

"How much?" Ray asked.

"A hundred and seventy thousand," Chili said.

"Listen, Chili," Ray said, "let's forget our little troubles, okay? What I did, what you did, that was a long time ago. This money, it's mine, right? You say nothing about it to anyone, and we stay friends."

"Okay with me," Chili said.

Ray Bones left with the key, and Chili picked up the phone. "The number for the airport police, please," he said.

"Who is this?" the policeman asked him when he called.

"I can't tell you," Chili said. "It's about that locker, C-018. The guy will be there soon. He's got an ugly white line in his head from a bullet. You can't miss him."

◆

Bo Catlett picked up the phone in his car and called the Bear for the third time, but there was still no answer. Where is that man? he thought. Did something go wrong? He put the phone down and got out of the car. This Karen Flores has a nice house, he thought.

Harry was there, waiting. "Any news?"

"He's your man, you tell me."

"He took the money and ran," Harry said.

"Or," Catlett said, "someone hit him on the head. Or the police are talking to him."

"No, the money's talking to him. I called his hotel. He's gone."

29

"The man's a thief, Harry. He robbed you."

"He robbed us," Harry said.

"No, Harry, he robbed you. It was your money. I gave you the key."

Harry looked at Bo with angry eyes. "What is this? I never saw that money and now I owe it to you?"

Catlett opened his hands and said, "You owe me something."

That's when Chili walked in. Bo Catlett talking, his hands in front of him. But he stood up as soon as he saw Chili.

"You were waiting for me? You talked to the Bear?" Chili asked. Let's finish this, Chili thought, you and me.

But Harry stood up too. Harry, always in the way, always talking. "I called and called. Where were you?"

"Talking to the police," Chili said, looking at Bo.

Catlett said, "The police got you but you're here?"

"Didn't have the key with me. Ask the Bear. He was there."

"You talk to him?" Catlett asked.

"He wanted me to give him back the key."

"He was trying to help you," Bo said. "The police wanted that key."

"The police were waiting for me."

"What can I say? You look like a gangster," Bo said.

"Really?" Chili began to take off his jacket. "Go now, Bo. Go quickly, before I hurt you. Before I clean the floor with your pretty clothes."

"You don't know me," Catlett said in a quiet voice. "You think you do, but you don't." He turned and walked out.

Harry looked at Chili and said, "Tell me again, you didn't get the money? But you still have the key, don't you?"

"There's more to it," Chili said, sitting down.

◆

Bo Catlett was sitting in his car in the street outside Karen Flores' house. Harry still needs money, he thought, so he still needs me. The door opened and Chili Palmer came out. Bo watched him. Palmer took a suitcase out of his car and walked

The door opened and Chili Palmer came out.
Bo watched him.

back in. What did Harry say? "No, I called his hotel. He's gone." He's not gone, Bo thought. He's staying with Karen now. Until I come back here and shoot him.

Chili was in the kitchen. She came in quietly. "Look at you," she said, "not worried about anything, are you?"

"Why worry?" he said.

"I spoke to Michael. He wants to see you."

"Wonderful. Let's tell Harry."

"No," Karen said, "he wants to see you, not Harry. Not about *Lovejoy*. You told him your idea, didn't you?"

"He wants to talk about that?" Chili was surprised.

"He wants to have dinner with you tonight, at *Jimmy's*."

"I don't know," Chili said. "Who pays?"

"You're laughing. You don't have a script," Karen said. "You have the beginning of an idea . . ."

"Oh, I have lots of ideas," Chili said. "But Harry has to come. We'll talk about *Lovejoy* too."

Harry walked in and Chili said "Michael called. He wants to talk."

"Well, it's about time," Harry said.

◆

Bo Catlett was out on the balcony of his house, high on a hill above Hollywood, looking down the mountain. He couldn't see the stones far below, but they were there. He looked over the railing into the black night and thought, fall off here and you die. In the movies, railings broke all the time, people fell through them. You couldn't fall through this railing. It was too strong. Too bad, he thought. He closed his eyes and saw Chili Palmer falling. That was an idea. He picked up the phone and called the Bear again. This time the Bear was home.

"Our man is too smart," the Bear said.

"Chili Palmer? Yeah, I heard."

"You saw the news? On television? The police caught a guy from Miami at the airport. Some gangster."

"Oh, you watching television instead of calling me?"

32

"I don't work for you now, Bo. I'm out of it."

"You hit your head when you fell down the stairs?" Bo asked.

"This guy is no Yayo. This guy is dangerous."

Catlett said "Listen, Bear, I had an idea. You come over here and work on my railing. Like they do in the movies. You understand? We get Chili Palmer here, he goes down the mountain. What do you think?'

"This isn't the movies, Bo. This guy is real."

"Yeah. Easier to go to the woman's house and kill him there. You're helping me."

There was silence, and then the Bear said, "No, I'm not. I told you, I'm not working for you now."

"I hate to hear that, Bear. Because if I get into trouble, I'll have to tell them about you. All about you."

There was silence again. The Bear said, "Why?" in a quiet voice.

"Because I'm not a nice guy," Bo said. "Why do you think?"

◆

Harry had the fish and Chili had a steak. Michael didn't like anything on the menu; movie stars never liked anything on the menu. He asked for an omelette.

They talked while they ate. Michael said, "It's a love story, really. They love each other. And when the gangster appears and their lives are in danger . . ."

"What gangster?" Harry asked.

Michael didn't answer the question. Instead he went on.

"And she's another man's wife. How do I feel about that? And what does her husband do? I mean, what's his job?"

"He's in the movie business," Chili said, "and his wife is a singer. We're still working on the end."

Harry was staring at Chili.

"You are?" Michael was surprised. "You haven't finished the script?"

"You read the script," Harry said. "I sent it to you."

33

"No you didn't," Michael said. He looked at his watch. "I have to go. But what I want, they have problems with the money. They don't feel right about keeping it."

"What money," Harry said, "are we talking about?"

"The three hundred thousand," Michael said, standing up. "What other money is there? And here's an idea. We see it on the bed, all of it. Make it a million – why not? And the shylock says . . ."

Harry said, "The shylock?"

Michael said, "Look at me, Harry."

Harry was already looking at him. Chili said, "That's good."

"You mean," Harry said, "all this time . . ."

Michael put out his hand. "Have to go. Chili, call me. Harry, be good." He walked away.

Harry threw his fork down on his plate. Chili took out a cigarette. He said, "Let's have a drink."

◆

They woke up in the middle of the night and Karen said, "Not again." Chili's eyes were still closed. She said, "It's Harry, downstairs. He's doing what you did. Go down and tell him to go home, Chili."

He said, "I don't think it's Harry."

Catlett sat in the dark, looking at the television. Just do it, he thought. Chili Palmer walks in, shoot him. No talk.

Chili put on his pants and shoes. He went to the door and stopped. He was listening. After a minute Karen said, "Are you going down?"

"I don't know."

"Then I will. You're as bad as Harry." She got out of bed.

"No, stay here. I think it's Catlett. Maybe Harry told Catlett about that first night."

Chili went downstairs.

Bo Catlett was tired of waiting. He left the room, walking quietly. He saw something on the stairs and he pointed the gun at it. Suddenly there was a scream. He'd never heard a scream

34

*Harry threw his fork down on his plate. Chili took out
a cigarette. He said, "Let's have a drink."*

that loud. He shot at the shape and it fell. The scream went on louder and louder, and he ran.

Chili stood up. "That was a great scream," he said. He remembered something. "Last night you said something about the Bear?"

"He called, his number's by the phone."

Chili talked to the Bear for a few minutes. When he finished, Karen said, "You're going to Catlett's house – why?"

"Remember Ray Bones? For twelve years I worried about that guy. I'm not doing that again."

◆

Bo Catlett heard a car outside his house. The police, he thought. But when he opened the door, the Bear was standing there.

"It's the middle of the night." He tried to look sleepy.

"I was here earlier, but you weren't. Take this." The Bear handed him Yayo's suitcase. "I came in but I didn't want to leave it here."

"You were in my house?"

"I just told you," the Bear said.

This was strange, Catlett thought. He said, "Bear, why are you talking to me like that. Aren't we friends?"

"Not the last time that we talked. You talked about the police."

"Hey, listen, I didn't mean it. I wasn't serious."

The Bear said "Really?"

Bo looked at the Bear. "Hey, Bear, you haven't asked me. Did I get Chili Palmer? Why not? Maybe you talked to him already. Bear, I'm glad you're here," he said, and left him and went into his bedroom. He took the gun from the table by his bed and put it in his pocket. And heard the second car.

◆

The door was open, so Chili walked in. Bo was coming out of another room. His hands were in the big pockets of his jacket. The Bear was standing between them. He moved to the side when Chili came in.

"People have tried to shoot me before, but I'm still here,"

"You like my balcony?" Bo asked, pulling the gun out of his pocket. "Let's all go see my balcony."

Chili said to Bo. "I'm here, and you, you're gone. Come near me, or Harry, again and I'll throw you off your pretty balcony."

"You like my balcony?" Bo asked, pulling the gun out of his pocket. "Let's all go see my balcony. You, too, Bear."

Outside, Chili said, "Okay, you win. The man with the gun is always right. I'll go back to Miami."

"No, you came to rob my house. Bear will tell them too, if Bear wants to live."

The Bear wanted to live. "Yeah, he came to rob you. And you didn't want to shoot. You said 'Stop' but he didn't. You came out here, he followed you. You have to see it, Bo, we have to do it like a movie. Then we can tell the police the same story, right?"

"Yeah, like a movie." Bo liked the idea.

"So he's here," the Bear said, holding Chili in his big arms, "and you go over there."

Bo went towards the railing. Chili tried to move, but he couldn't. The Bear was too strong. "And you're holding the railing when you shoot," the Bear said.

Bo pointed the gun straight at Chili's jumping heart and put his other hand on the railing. And screamed when the railing fell away behind him. One minute Catlett was there and the next minute he wasn't. When he hit the stones, he was still thinking, "Like a movie."

The Bear let go of Chili. "It was his idea," he said.

◆

Chili, Michael, Harry and Karen were talking about Chili's movie. Chili was saying, "At the end, the guy falls off a balcony."

Michael said, "I love the story, but the end . . . ? Maybe I can shoot him or something."

Chili said, "Michael, look at me."

Michael smiled. "Yeah, I've got those cold eyes now."

"No, Michael, it's not that. When I see the shylock, I don't see you."

Harry bit his lips. Please don't, he thought.

"You don't?" Michael asked, surprised. "Why not?"

Chili looked at the actor. "You're too short," he said.

ACTIVITIES

Pages 1–12

Before you read

1   Look at the picture on the front cover of the book. You are at a party and you see these four people. Which of them do you want to meet? Which of them do you not want to talk to? Why?

2   Find these words in your dictionary.
    cab gangster mad owe scared script
    Which of them is
    a   something you read?   **b**   something you ride in?
    c   something you feel?   **d**   something you do with money?
    e   a criminal?

After you read

3   Make correct sentences.
    a   Chili Palmer   puts money into movies.
    b   Ray Bones   wants money to make movies.
    c   Karen Flores   works for Jimmy Cap.
    d   Harry Zimm   lives in Las Vegas.
    e   Leo Devoe   was married to somebody famous.
    f   Bo Catlett   lends people money.
    g   Dick Allen   wants people to think he is dead.

4   How are these important to the story?
    a $150,000   **b** $300,000   **c** $500,000

5   How are these people useful to Harry Zimm?
    a   Chili Palmer   **b**   Bo Catlett   **c**   Karen Flores

6   Why does a film-maker like Harry Zimm work with gangsters, do you think? Why doesn't he borrow money from his bank?

7   Work in pairs. Act out this conversation between Chili Palmer and Dick Allen.

Student A: You are Dick Allen. You want Chili to find Harry Zimm and your money. Tell him everything he needs to know.

Student B: You are Chili. Ask Allen about your new job.

Pages 12–26

Before you read

8 Will Bo Catlett be pleased to meet Chili Palmer again, do you think? Why, or why not?

9 Find these words in your dictionary.

locker stuntman

a Think of *three* places where people keep *lockers*.

b Think of *three* things in movies that stuntmen do.

After you read

10 Choose the correct answer.

   a Bo Catlett goes to Harry's office

     (i) because Chili calls him.

     (ii) to read a script.

     (iii) to find out who Chili is.

   b Bo doesn't give Yayo the money because

     (i) he hasn't got it.

     (ii) he's planning to shoot him.

     (iii) he can't get to it.

   c Michael Weir's eyes turn cold because

     (i) he's acting

     (ii) he doesn't want to talk about the movie.

     (iii) he realizes that Chili is a gangster.

   d Bo doesn't want to kill Chili because

     (i) Bear doesn't want him to.

     (ii) Chili has dangerous friends.

     (iii) he thinks Chili will be useful.

11 What do the underlined words mean?

   a Not Nicki <u>then</u> (page 14)

   b "How are you doing <u>that</u>?" (page 16)

c "You've done <u>this</u> before." (page 17)

d Bo liked <u>that</u>. (page 24)

12 How are these important to the story?

  a the key to a locker   **b** a newspaper   **c** Tommy

Pages 26–38

Before you read

13 Chili promises to bring Harry the money from the airport. Is Harry right to believe him, do you think? Why, or why not?

14 Find these words in your dictionary.

  balcony railing

  Use both words in *one* sentence.

After you read

15 Who says or thinks these words, about whom and why?

  a stupid   **c** a gangster   **e** not a nice guy

  b a thief   **d** too smart   **f** too short

16 Who says these things, and what do they mean?

  a "Not again."   **c** "Like a movie."

  b "You mean, all this time . . ."

17 How does Bear help Chili in the end? Why does he do it?

Writing

18 Before people write scripts, they write a short description of their movie idea. Think about a movie you've seen. Write down the general idea of the story, and the important things that happen.

19 On the last page, Michael says: "I love the story, but the end . . . ?" Choose a famous story from your own country and write a new ending for it.

20 You are Bones. The police promise to free you if you tell them everything about the key and the money in the locker. Write a report for them.

21 You are Leo Devoe. Write a letter to your wife and tell her about your new life without her.

Answers for the Activities in this book are published in our free resource packs for teachers, the Penguin Readers Factsheets, or available on a separate sheet. Please write to your local Pearson Education office or to: Marketing Department, Penguin Longman Publishing, 5 Bentinck Street, London W1M 5RN.